Love Songs

Sara Teasdale

Contents

LOVE SONGS

BY

Sara Teasdale

To E.

I have remembered beauty in the night,
 Against black silences I waked to see
 A shower of sunlight over Italy
And green Ravello dreaming on her height;
I have remembered music in the dark,
 The clean swift brightness of a fugue of Bach's,
 And running water singing on the rocks
When once in English woods I heard a lark.

But all remembered beauty is no more
 Than a vague prelude to the thought of you--
 You are the rarest soul I ever knew,
   Lover of beauty, knightliest and best;
My thoughts seek you as waves that seek the shore,
   And when I think of you, I am at rest.

I

Barter

Life has loveliness to sell,
 All beautiful and splendid things,
Blue waves whitened on a cliff,
 Soaring fire that sways and sings,
And children's faces looking up
Holding wonder like a cup.

Life has loveliness to sell,
 Music like a curve of gold,
Scent of pine trees in the rain,
 Eyes that love you, arms that hold,
And for your spirit's still delight,
Holy thoughts that star the night.

Spend all you have for loveliness,
 Buy it and never count the cost;
For one white singing hour of peace
 Count many a year of strife well lost,
And for a breath of ecstasy
Give all you have been, or could be.

Twilight

Dreamily over the roofs
 The cold spring rain is falling;
Out in the lonely tree
 A bird is calling, calling.

Slowly over the earth
 The wings of night are falling;
My heart like the bird in the tree
 Is calling, calling, calling.

Night Song at Amalfi

I asked the heaven of stars
 What I should give my love--
It answered me with silence,
 Silence above.

I asked the darkened sea
 Down where the fishers go--
It answered me with silence,
 Silence below.

Oh, I could give him weeping,
 Or I could give him song--

But how can I give silence,
  My whole life long?

The Look

Strephon kissed me in the spring,
  Robin in the fall,
But Colin only looked at me
  And never kissed at all.

Strephon's kiss was lost in jest,
  Robin's lost in play,
But the kiss in Colin's eyes
  Haunts me night and day.

A Winter Night

My window-pane is starred with frost,
  The world is bitter cold to-night,
The moon is cruel, and the wind
  Is like a two-edged sword to smite.

God pity all the homeless ones,
  The beggars pacing to and fro,

God pity all the poor to-night
 Who walk the lamp-lit streets of snow.

My room is like a bit of June,
 Warm and close-curtained fold on fold,
But somewhere, like a homeless child,
 My heart is crying in the cold.

A Cry

Oh, there are eyes that he can see,
 And hands to make his hands rejoice,
But to my lover I must be
 Only a voice.

Oh, there are breasts to bear his head,
 And lips whereon his lips can lie,
But I must be till I am dead
 Only a cry.

Gifts

I gave my first love laughter,
 I gave my second tears,

I gave my third love silence
　Through all the years.

My first love gave me singing,
　My second eyes to see,
But oh, it was my third love
　Who gave my soul to me.

But Not to Me

The April night is still and sweet
　With flowers on every tree;
Peace comes to them on quiet feet,
　　But not to me.

My peace is hidden in his breast
　Where I shall never be;
Love comes to-night to all the rest,
　　But not to me.

Song at Capri

When beauty grows too great to bear
 How shall I ease me of its ache,
For beauty more than bitterness
 Makes the heart break.

Now while I watch the dreaming sea
 With isles like flowers against her breast,
Only one voice in all the world
 Could give me rest.

Child, Child

Child, child, love while you can
The voice and the eyes and the soul of a man;
Never fear though it break your heart--
Out of the wound new joy will start;
Only love proudly and gladly and well,
Though love be heaven or love be hell.

Child, child, love while you may,
For life is short as a happy day;
Never fear the thing you feel--
Only by love is life made real;
Love, for the deadly sins are seven,

Only through love will you enter heaven.

Love Me

Brown-thrush singing all day long
 In the leaves above me,
Take my love this April song,
 "Love me, love me, love me!"

When he harkens what you say,
 Bid him, lest he miss me,
Leave his work or leave his play,
 And kiss me, kiss me, kiss me!

Pierrot

Pierrot stands in the garden
 Beneath a waning moon,
And on his lute he fashions
 A fragile silver tune.

Pierrot plays in the garden,
 He thinks he plays for me,
But I am quite forgotten

Under the cherry tree.

Pierrot plays in the garden,
 And all the roses know
That Pierrot loves his music,--
 But I love Pierrot.

Wild Asters

In the spring I asked the daisies
 If his words were true,
And the clever, clear-eyed daisies
 Always knew.

Now the fields are brown and barren,
 Bitter autumn blows,
And of all the stupid asters
 Not one knows.

The Song for Colin

I sang a song at dusking time
 Beneath the evening star,
And Terence left his latest rhyme

To answer from afar.

Pierrot laid down his lute to weep,
 And sighed, "She sings for me."
But Colin slept a careless sleep
 Beneath an apple tree.

Four Winds

"Four winds blowing through the sky,
You have seen poor maidens die,
Tell me then what I shall do
That my lover may be true."
Said the wind from out the south,
"Lay no kiss upon his mouth,"
And the wind from out the west,
"Wound the heart within his breast,"
And the wind from out the east,
"Send him empty from the feast,"
And the wind from out the north,
"In the tempest thrust him forth;
When thou art more cruel than he,
Then will Love be kind to thee."

Debt

What do I owe to you
 Who loved me deep and long?
You never gave my spirit wings
 Or gave my heart a song.

But oh, to him I loved,
 Who loved me not at all,
I owe the open gate
 That led through heaven's wall.

Faults

They came to tell your faults to me,
They named them over one by one;
I laughed aloud when they were done,
I knew them all so well before,--
Oh, they were blind, too blind to see
Your faults had made me love you more.

Buried Love

I have come to bury Love
 Beneath a tree,
In the forest tall and black
 Where none can see.

I shall put no flowers at his head,
 Nor stone at his feet,
For the mouth I loved so much
 Was bittersweet.

I shall go no more to his grave,
 For the woods are cold.
I shall gather as much of joy
 As my hands can hold.

I shall stay all day in the sun
 Where the wide winds blow,--
But oh, I shall cry at night
 When none will know.

The Fountain

All through the deep blue night
 The fountain sang alone;
It sang to the drowsy heart
 Of the satyr carved in stone.

The fountain sang and sang,
 But the satyr never stirred--
Only the great white moon
 In the empty heaven heard.

The fountain sang and sang
 While on the marble rim
The milk-white peacocks slept,
 And their dreams were strange and dim.

Bright dew was on the grass,
 And on the ilex, dew,
The dreamy milk-white birds
 Were all a-glisten, too.

The fountain sang and sang
 The things one cannot tell;
The dreaming peacocks stirred
 And the gleaming dew-drops fell.

I Shall Not Care

When I am dead and over me bright April
 Shakes out her rain-drenched hair,
Though you should lean above me broken-hearted,
 I shall not care.

I shall have peace, as leafy trees are peaceful
 When rain bends down the bough,
And I shall be more silent and cold-hearted
 Than you are now.

After Parting

Oh, I have sown my love so wide
 That he will find it everywhere;
It will awake him in the night,
 It will enfold him in the air.

I set my shadow in his sight
 And I have winged it with desire,
That it may be a cloud by day,
 And in the night a shaft of fire.

A Prayer

Until I lose my soul and lie
 Blind to the beauty of the earth,
Deaf though shouting wind goes by,
 Dumb in a storm of mirth;

Until my heart is quenched at length
 And I have left the land of men,
Oh, let me love with all my strength
 Careless if I am loved again.

Spring Night

The park is filled with night and fog,
 The veils are drawn about the world,
The drowsy lights along the paths
 Are dim and pearled.

Gold and gleaming the empty streets,
 Gold and gleaming the misty lake,
The mirrored lights like sunken swords,
 Glimmer and shake.

Oh, is it not enough to be
Here with this beauty over me?

My throat should ache with praise, and I
Should kneel in joy beneath the sky.
O, beauty, are you not enough?
Why am I crying after love,
With youth, a singing voice, and eyes
To take earth's wonder with surprise?

Why have I put off my pride,
Why am I unsatisfied,--
I, for whom the pensive night
Binds her cloudy hair with light,--
I, for whom all beauty burns
Like incense in a million urns?
O beauty, are you not enough?
Why am I crying after love?

May Wind

I said, "I have shut my heart
 As one shuts an open door,
That Love may starve therein
 And trouble me no more."

But over the roofs there came
 The wet new wind of May,
And a tune blew up from the curb
 Where the street-pianos play.

My room was white with the sun

And Love cried out in me,
"I am strong, I will break your heart
Unless you set me free."

Tides

Love in my heart was a fresh tide flowing
 Where the starlike sea gulls soar;
The sun was keen and the foam was blowing
 High on the rocky shore.

But now in the dusk the tide is turning,
 Lower the sea gulls soar,
And the waves that rose in resistless yearning
 Are broken forevermore.

After Love

There is no magic any more,
 We meet as other people do,
You work no miracle for me
 Nor I for you.

You were the wind and I the sea--

There is no splendor any more,
I have grown listless as the pool
  Beside the shore.

But though the pool is safe from storm
  And from the tide has found surcease,
It grows more bitter than the sea,
  For all its peace.

New Love and Old

In my heart the old love
  Struggled with the new;
It was ghostly waking
  All night through.

Dear things, kind things,
  That my old love said,
Ranged themselves reproachfully
  Round my bed.

But I could not heed them,
  For I seemed to see
The eyes of my new love
  Fixed on me.

Old love, old love,
  How can I be true?
Shall I be faithless to myself
  Or to you?

The Kiss

I hoped that he would love me,
 And he has kissed my mouth,
But I am like a stricken bird
 That cannot reach the south.

For though I know he loves me,
 To-night my heart is sad;
His kiss was not so wonderful
 As all the dreams I had.

Swans

Night is over the park, and a few brave stars
 Look on the lights that link it with chains of gold,
The lake bears up their reflection in broken bars
 That seem too heavy for tremulous water to hold.

We watch the swans that sleep in a shadowy place,
 And now and again one wakes and uplifts its head;
How still you are--your gaze is on my face--
 We watch the swans and never a word is said.

The River

I came from the sunny valleys
 And sought for the open sea,
For I thought in its gray expanses
 My peace would come to me.

I came at last to the ocean
 And found it wild and black,
And I cried to the windless valleys,
 "Be kind and take me back!"

But the thirsty tide ran inland,
 And the salt waves drank of me,
And I who was fresh as the rainfall
 Am bitter as the sea.

November

The world is tired, the year is old,
 The fading leaves are glad to die,
The wind goes shivering with cold
 Where the brown reeds are dry.

Our love is dying like the grass,
 And we who kissed grow coldly kind,

Half glad to see our old love pass
 Like leaves along the wind.

Spring Rain

I thought I had forgotten,
 But it all came back again
To-night with the first spring thunder
 In a rush of rain.

I remembered a darkened doorway
 Where we stood while the storm swept by,
Thunder gripping the earth
 And lightning scrawled on the sky.

The passing motor busses swayed,
 For the street was a river of rain,
Lashed into little golden waves
 In the lamp light's stain.

With the wild spring rain and thunder
 My heart was wild and gay;
Your eyes said more to me that night
 Than your lips would ever say. . . .

I thought I had forgotten,
 But it all came back again
To-night with the first spring thunder
 In a rush of rain.

The Ghost

I went back to the clanging city,
 I went back where my old loves stayed,
But my heart was full of my new love's glory,
 My eyes were laughing and unafraid.

I met one who had loved me madly
 And told his love for all to hear--
But we talked of a thousand things together,
 The past was buried too deep to fear.

I met the other, whose love was given
 With never a kiss and scarcely a word--
Oh, it was then the terror took me
 Of words unuttered that breathed and stirred.

Oh, love that lives its life with laughter
 Or love that lives its life with tears
Can die--but love that is never spoken
 Goes like a ghost through the winding years. . . .

I went back to the clanging city,
 I went back where my old loves stayed,
My heart was full of my new love's glory,--
 But my eyes were suddenly afraid.

Summer Night, Riverside

In the wild, soft summer darkness
How many and many a night we two together
Sat in the park and watched the Hudson
Wearing her lights like golden spangles
Glinting on black satin.
The rail along the curving pathway
Was low in a happy place to let us cross,
And down the hill a tree that dripped with bloom
Sheltered us,
While your kisses and the flowers,
Falling, falling,
Tangled my hair. . . .

The frail white stars moved slowly over the sky.

And now, far off
In the fragrant darkness
The tree is tremulous again with bloom,
For June comes back.

To-night what girl
Dreamily before her mirror shakes from her hair
This year's blossoms, clinging in its coils?

Jewels

If I should see your eyes again,
 I know how far their look would go--
Back to a morning in the park
 With sapphire shadows on the snow.

Or back to oak trees in the spring
 When you unloosed my hair and kissed
The head that lay against your knees
 In the leaf shadow's amethyst.

And still another shining place
 We would remember--how the dun
Wild mountain held us on its crest
 One diamond morning white with sun.

But I will turn my eyes from you
 As women turn to put away
The jewels they have worn at night
 And cannot wear in sober day.

II
Interlude: Songs out of Sorrow

I. Spirit's House

From naked stones of agony
I will build a house for me;
As a mason all alone
I will raise it, stone by stone,
And every stone where I have bled
Will show a sign of dusky red.
I have not gone the way in vain,
For I have good of all my pain;
My spirit's quiet house will be
Built of naked stones I trod
On roads where I lost sight of God.

II. Mastery

I would not have a god come in
To shield me suddenly from sin,
And set my house of life to rights;
Nor angels with bright burning wings
Ordering my earthly thoughts and things;
Rather my own frail guttering lights
Wind blown and nearly beaten out;
Rather the terror of the nights
And long, sick groping after doubt;
Rather be lost than let my soul
Slip vaguely from my own control--
Of my own spirit let me be
In sole though feeble mastery.

III. Lessons

Unless I learn to ask no help
 From any other soul but mine,
To seek no strength in waving reeds
 Nor shade beneath a straggling pine;
Unless I learn to look at Grief
 Unshrinking from her tear-blind eyes,
And take from Pleasure fearlessly
 Whatever gifts will make me wise--

Unless I learn these things on earth,
Why was I ever given birth?

IV. Wisdom

When I have ceased to break my wings
Against the faultiness of things,
And learned that compromises wait
Behind each hardly opened gate,
When I can look Life in the eyes,
Grown calm and very coldly wise,
Life will have given me the Truth,
And taken in exchange--my youth.

V. In a Burying Ground

This is the spot where I will lie
 When life has had enough of me,
These are the grasses that will blow
 Above me like a living sea.

These gay old lilies will not shrink
 To draw their life from death of mine,
And I will give my body's fire

To make blue flowers on this vine.

"O Soul," I said, "have you no tears?
 Was not the body dear to you?"
I heard my soul say carelessly,
 "The myrtle flowers will grow more blue."

VI. Wood Song

I heard a wood thrush in the dusk
 Twirl three notes and make a star--
My heart that walked with bitterness
 Came back from very far.

Three shining notes were all he had,
 And yet they made a starry call--
I caught life back against my breast
 And kissed it, scars and all.

VII. Refuge

From my spirit's gray defeat,
From my pulse's flagging beat,
From my hopes that turned to sand

Sifting through my close-clenched hand,
From my own fault's slavery,
If I can sing, I still am free.

For with my singing I can make
A refuge for my spirit's sake,
A house of shining words, to be
My fragile immortality.

III

The Flight

Look back with longing eyes and know that I will follow,
Lift me up in your love as a light wind lifts a swallow,
Let our flight be far in sun or blowing rain--
But what if I heard my first love calling me again?

Hold me on your heart as the brave sea holds the foam,
Take me far away to the hills that hide your home;
Peace shall thatch the roof and love shall latch the door--
But what if I heard my first love calling me once more?

Dew

As dew leaves the cobweb lightly
 Threaded with stars,
Scattering jewels on the fence

And the pasture bars;
As dawn leaves the dry grass bright
 And the tangled weeds
Bearing a rainbow gem
 On each of their seeds;
So has your love, my lover,
 Fresh as the dawn,
Made me a shining road
 To travel on,
Set every common sight
 Of tree or stone
Delicately alight
 For me alone.

To-night

The moon is a curving flower of gold,
 The sky is still and blue;
The moon was made for the sky to hold,
 And I for you.

The moon is a flower without a stem,
 The sky is luminous;
Eternity was made for them,
 To-night for us.

Ebb Tide

When the long day goes by
 And I do not see your face,
The old wild, restless sorrow
 Steals from its hiding place.

My day is barren and broken,
 Bereft of light and song,
A sea beach bleak and windy
 That moans the whole day long.

To the empty beach at ebb tide,
 Bare with its rocks and scars,
Come back like the sea with singing,
 And light of a million stars.

I Would Live in Your Love

I would live in your love as the sea-grasses live in the sea,
Borne up by each wave as it passes, drawn down by each wave that recedes;
I would empty my soul of the dreams that have gathered in me,
I would beat with your heart as it beats, I would follow your soul
 as it leads.

Because

Oh, because you never tried
To bow my will or break my pride,
And nothing of the cave-man made
You want to keep me half afraid,
Nor ever with a conquering air
You thought to draw me unaware--
Take me, for I love you more
Than I ever loved before.

And since the body's maidenhood
Alone were neither rare nor good
Unless with it I gave to you
A spirit still untrammeled, too,
Take my dreams and take my mind
That were masterless as wind;
And "Master!" I shall say to you
Since you never asked me to.

The Tree of Song

I sang my songs for the rest,
 For you I am still;
The tree of my song is bare
 On its shining hill.

For you came like a lordly wind,
  And the leaves were whirled
Far as forgotten things
  Past the rim of the world.

The tree of my song stands bare
  Against the blue--
I gave my songs to the rest,
  Myself to you.

The Giver

You bound strong sandals on my feet,
  You gave me bread and wine,
And sent me under sun and stars,
  For all the world was mine.

Oh, take the sandals off my feet,
  You know not what you do;
For all my world is in your arms,
  My sun and stars are you.

April Song

Willow, in your April gown
 Delicate and gleaming,
Do you mind in years gone by
 All my dreaming?

Spring was like a call to me
 That I could not answer,
I was chained to loneliness,
 I, the dancer.

Willow, twinkling in the sun,
 Still your leaves and hear me,
I can answer spring at last,
 Love is near me!

The Wanderer

I saw the sunset-colored sands,
 The Nile like flowing fire between,
 Where Rameses stares forth serene,
And Ammon's heavy temple stands.

I saw the rocks where long ago,
 Above the sea that cries and breaks,

Swift Perseus with Medusa's snakes
Set free the maiden white like snow.

And many skies have covered me,
 And many winds have blown me forth,
 And I have loved the green, bright north,
And I have loved the cold, sweet sea.

But what to me are north and south,
 And what the lure of many lands,
 Since you have leaned to catch my hands
And lay a kiss upon my mouth.

The Years

To-night I close my eyes and see
A strange procession passing me--
The years before I saw your face
Go by me with a wistful grace;
They pass, the sensitive, shy years,
As one who strives to dance, half blind with tears.

The years went by and never knew
That each one brought me nearer you;
Their path was narrow and apart
And yet it led me to your heart--
Oh, sensitive, shy years, oh, lonely years,
That strove to sing with voices drowned in tears.

Enough

It is enough for me by day
 To walk the same bright earth with him;
Enough that over us by night
 The same great roof of stars is dim.

I do not hope to bind the wind
 Or set a fetter on the sea--
It is enough to feel his love
 Blow by like music over me.

Come

Come, when the pale moon like a petal
 Floats in the pearly dusk of spring,
Come with arms outstretched to take me,
 Come with lips pursed up to cling.

Come, for life is a frail moth flying,
 Caught in the web of the years that pass,
And soon we two, so warm and eager,
 Will be as the gray stones in the grass.

Joy

I am wild, I will sing to the trees,
 I will sing to the stars in the sky,
I love, I am loved, he is mine,
 Now at last I can die!

I am sandaled with wind and with flame,
 I have heart-fire and singing to give,
I can tread on the grass or the stars,
 Now at last I can live!

Riches

I have no riches but my thoughts,
 Yet these are wealth enough for me;
My thoughts of you are golden coins
 Stamped in the mint of memory;

And I must spend them all in song,
 For thoughts, as well as gold, must be
Left on the hither side of death
 To gain their immortality.

Dusk in War Time

A half-hour more and you will lean
 To gather me close in the old sweet way--
But oh, to the woman over the sea
 Who will come at the close of day?

A half-hour more and I will hear
 The key in the latch and the strong, quick tread--
But oh, the woman over the sea
 Waiting at dusk for one who is dead!

Peace

Peace flows into me
 As the tide to the pool by the shore;
 It is mine forevermore,
It will not ebb like the sea.

I am the pool of blue
 That worships the vivid sky;
 My hopes were heaven-high,
They are all fulfilled in you.

I am the pool of gold
 When sunset burns and dies--

You are my deepening skies;
Give me your stars to hold.

Moods

I am the still rain falling,
 Too tired for singing mirth--
Oh, be the green fields calling,
 Oh, be for me the earth!

I am the brown bird pining
 To leave the nest and fly--
Oh, be the fresh cloud shining,
 Oh, be for me the sky!

Houses of Dreams

You took my empty dreams
 And filled them every one
With tenderness and nobleness,
 April and the sun.

The old empty dreams
 Where my thoughts would throng

Are far too full of happiness
 To even hold a song.

Oh, the empty dreams were dim
 And the empty dreams were wide,
They were sweet and shadowy houses
 Where my thoughts could hide.

But you took my dreams away
 And you made them all come true--
My thoughts have no place now to play,
 And nothing now to do.

Lights

When we come home at night and close the door,
 Standing together in the shadowy room,
 Safe in our own love and the gentle gloom,
Glad of familiar wall and chair and floor,

Glad to leave far below the clanging city;
 Looking far downward to the glaring street
 Gaudy with light, yet tired with many feet,
In both of us wells up a wordless pity;

Men have tried hard to put away the dark;
 A million lighted windows brilliantly
   Inlay with squares of gold the winter night,
But to us standing here there comes the stark

Sense of the lives behind each yellow light,
And not one wholly joyous, proud, or free.

"I Am Not Yours"

I am not yours, not lost in you,
 Not lost, although I long to be
Lost as a candle lit at noon,
 Lost as a snowflake in the sea.

You love me, and I find you still
 A spirit beautiful and bright,
Yet I am I, who long to be
 Lost as a light is lost in light.

Oh plunge me deep in love--put out
 My senses, leave me deaf and blind,
Swept by the tempest of your love,
 A taper in a rushing wind.

Doubt

My soul lives in my body's house,
 And you have both the house and her--
But sometimes she is less your own
 Than a wild, gay adventurer;
A restless and an eager wraith,
 How can I tell what she will do--
Oh, I am sure of my body's faith,
 But what if my soul broke faith with you?

The Wind

A wind is blowing over my soul,
 I hear it cry the whole night through--
Is there no peace for me on earth
 Except with you?

Alas, the wind has made me wise,
 Over my naked soul it blew,--
There is no peace for me on earth
 Even with you.

Morning

I went out on an April morning
 All alone, for my heart was high,
I was a child of the shining meadow,
 I was a sister of the sky.

There in the windy flood of morning
 Longing lifted its weight from me,
Lost as a sob in the midst of cheering,
 Swept as a sea-bird out to sea.

Other Men

When I talk with other men
 I always think of you--
Your words are keener than their words,
 And they are gentler, too.

When I look at other men,
 I wish your face were there,
With its gray eyes and dark skin
 And tossed black hair.

When I think of other men,
 Dreaming alone by day,

The thought of you like a strong wind
 Blows the dreams away.

Embers

I said, "My youth is gone
 Like a fire beaten out by the rain,
That will never sway and sing
 Or play with the wind again."

I said, "It is no great sorrow
 That quenched my youth in me,
But only little sorrows
 Beating ceaselessly."

I thought my youth was gone,
 But you returned--
Like a flame at the call of the wind
 It leaped and burned;

Threw off its ashen cloak,
 And gowned anew
Gave itself like a bride
 Once more to you.

Message

I heard a cry in the night,
 A thousand miles it came,
Sharp as a flash of light,
 My name, my name!

It was your voice I heard,
 You waked and loved me so--
I send you back this word,
 I know, I know!

The Lamp

If I can bear your love like a lamp before me,
When I go down the long steep Road of Darkness,
I shall not fear the everlasting shadows,
  Nor cry in terror.

If I can find out God, then I shall find Him,
If none can find Him, then I shall sleep soundly,
Knowing how well on earth your love sufficed me,
  A lamp in darkness.

IV

A November Night

There! See the line of lights,
A chain of stars down either side the street--
Why can't you lift the chain and give it to me,
A necklace for my throat? I'd twist it round
And you could play with it. You smile at me
As though I were a little dreamy child
Behind whose eyes the fairies live. . . . And see,
The people on the street look up at us
All envious. We are a king and queen,
Our royal carriage is a motor bus,
We watch our subjects with a haughty joy. . . .
How still you are! Have you been hard at work
And are you tired to-night? It is so long
Since I have seen you--four whole days, I think.
My heart is crowded full of foolish thoughts
Like early flowers in an April meadow,
And I must give them to you, all of them,
Before they fade. The people I have met,
The play I saw, the trivial, shifting things
That loom too big or shrink too little, shadows

That hurry, gesturing along a wall,
Haunting or gay--and yet they all grow real
And take their proper size here in my heart
When you have seen them. . . . There's the Plaza now,
A lake of light! To-night it almost seems
That all the lights are gathered in your eyes,
Drawn somehow toward you. See the open park
Lying below us with a million lamps
Scattered in wise disorder like the stars.
We look down on them as God must look down
On constellations floating under Him
Tangled in clouds. . . . Come, then, and let us walk
Since we have reached the park. It is our garden,
All black and blossomless this winter night,
But we bring April with us, you and I;
We set the whole world on the trail of spring.
I think that every path we ever took
Has marked our footprints in mysterious fire,
Delicate gold that only fairies see.
When they wake up at dawn in hollow tree-trunks
And come out on the drowsy park, they look
Along the empty paths and say, "Oh, here
They went, and here, and here, and here! Come, see,
Here is their bench, take hands and let us dance
About it in a windy ring and make
A circle round it only they can cross
When they come back again!" . . . Look at the lake--
Do you remember how we watched the swans
That night in late October while they slept?
Swans must have stately dreams, I think. But now
The lake bears only thin reflected lights
That shake a little. How I long to take
One from the cold black water--new-made gold

To give you in your hand! And see, and see,
There is a star, deep in the lake, a star!
Oh, dimmer than a pearl--if you stoop down
Your hand could almost reach it up to me. . . .

There was a new frail yellow moon to-night--
I wish you could have had it for a cup
With stars like dew to fill it to the brim. . . .

How cold it is! Even the lights are cold;
They have put shawls of fog around them, see!
What if the air should grow so dimly white
That we would lose our way along the paths
Made new by walls of moving mist receding
The more we follow. . . . What a silver night!
That was our bench the time you said to me
The long new poem--but how different now,
How eerie with the curtain of the fog
Making it strange to all the friendly trees!
There is no wind, and yet great curving scrolls
Carve themselves, ever changing, in the mist.
Walk on a little, let me stand here watching
To see you, too, grown strange to me and far. . . .
I used to wonder how the park would be
If one night we could have it all alone--
No lovers with close arm-encircled waists
To whisper and break in upon our dreams.
And now we have it! Every wish comes true!
We are alone now in a fleecy world;
Even the stars have gone. We two alone!

The Codes Of Hammurabi And Moses
W. W. Davies

QTY

The discovery of the Hammurabi Code is one of the greatest achievements of archaeology, and is of paramount interest, not only to the student of the Bible, but also to all those interested in ancient history...

Religion   **ISBN: *1-59462-338-4***   **Pages:132**
MSRP $12.95

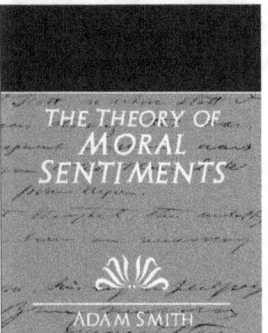

The Theory of Moral Sentiments
Adam Smith

QTY

This work from 1749. contains original theories of conscience amd moral judgment and it is the foundation for systemof morals.

Philosophy ISBN: *1-59462-777-0*   **Pages:536**
MSRP $19.95

Jessica's First Prayer
Hesba Stretton

QTY

In a screened and secluded corner of one of the many railway-bridges which span the streets of London there could be seen a few years ago, from five o'clock every morning until half past eight, a tidily set-out coffee-stall, consisting of a trestle and board, upon which stood two large tin cans, with a small fire of charcoal burning under each so as to keep the coffee boiling during the early hours of the morning when the work-people were thronging into the city on their way to their daily toil...

Pages:84

Childrens   ISBN: *1-59462-373-2*   *MSRP $9.95*

My Life and Work
Henry Ford

QTY

Henry Ford revolutionized the world with his implementation of mass production for the Model T automobile. Gain valuable business insight into his life and work with his own auto-biography... "We have only started on our development of our country we have not as yet, with all our talk of wonderful progress, done more than scratch the surface. The progress has been wonderful enough but..."

Pages:300

Biographies/   ISBN: *1-59462-198-5*   *MSRP $21.95*

The Art of Cross-Examination
Francis Wellman

QTY

I presume it is the experience of every author, after his first book is published upon an important subject, to be almost overwhelmed with a wealth of ideas and illustrations which could readily have been included in his book, and which to his own mind, at least, seem to make a second edition inevitable. Such certainly was the case with me; and when the first edition had reached its sixth impression in five months, I rejoiced to learn that it seemed to my publishers that the book had met with a sufficiently favorable reception to justify a second and considerably enlarged edition. ..

Pages:412

Reference   ISBN: *1-59462-647-2*   *MSRP $19.95*

On the Duty of Civil Disobedience
Henry David Thoreau

QTY

Thoreau wrote his famous essay, On the Duty of Civil Disobedience, as a protest against an unjust but popular war and the immoral but popular institution of slave-owning. He did more than write—he declined to pay his taxes, and was hauled off to gaol in consequence. Who can say how much this refusal of his hastened the end of the war and of slavery ?

Law   ISBN: *1-59462-747-9*   **Pages:48**

MSRP $7.45

Dream Psychology Psychoanalysis for Beginners
Sigmund Freud

QTY

Sigmund Freud, born Sigismund Schlomo Freud (May 6, 1856 - September 23, 1939), was a Jewish-Austrian neurologist and psychiatrist who co-founded the psychoanalytic school of psychology. Freud is best known for his theories of the unconscious mind, especially involving the mechanism of repression; his redefinition of sexual desire as mobile and directed towards a wide variety of objects; and his therapeutic techniques, especially his understanding of transference in the therapeutic relationship and the presumed value of dreams as sources of insight into unconscious desires.

Pages:196

Psychology   ISBN: *1-59462-905-6*   *MSRP $15.45*

The Miracle of Right Thought
Orison Swett Marden

QTY

Believe with all of your heart that you will do what you were made to do. When the mind has once formed the habit of holding cheerful, happy, prosperous pictures, it will not be easy to form the opposite habit. It does not matter how improbable or how far away this realization may see, or how dark the prospects may be, if we visualize them as best we can, as vividly as possible, hold tenaciously to them and vigorously struggle to attain them, they will gradually become actualized, realized in the life. But a desire, a longing without endeavor, a yearning abandoned or held indifferently will vanish without realization.

Pages:360

Self Help   ISBN: *1-59462-644-8*   *MSRP $25.45*

QTY

The Rosicrucian Cosmo-Conception Mystic Christianity *by Max Heindel* ISBN: *1-59462-188-8* **$38.95**
The Rosicrucian Cosmo-conception is not dogmatic, neither does it appeal to any other authority than the reason of the student. It is: not controversial, but is: sent forth in the, hope that it may help to clear... New Age/Religion Pages 646

Abandonment To Divine Providence *by Jean-Pierre de Caussade* ISBN: *1-59462-228-0* **$25.95**
"The Rev. Jean Pierre de Caussade was one of the most remarkable spiritual writers of the Society of Jesus in France in the 18th Century. His death took place at Toulouse in 1751. His works have gone through many editions and have been republished... Inspirational/Religion Pages 400

Mental Chemistry *by Charles Haanel* ISBN: *1-59462-192-6* **$23.95**
Mental Chemistry allows the change of material conditions by combining and appropriately utilizing the power of the mind. Much like applied chemistry creates something new and unique out of careful combinations of chemicals the mastery of mental chemistry... New Age Pages 354

The Letters of Robert Browning and Elizabeth Barret Barrett 1845-1846 vol II ISBN: *1-59462-193-4* **$35.95**
by Robert Browning and Elizabeth Barrett Biographies Pages 596

Gleanings In Genesis (volume I) *by Arthur W. Pink* ISBN: *1-59462-130-6* **$27.45**
Appropriately has Genesis been termed "the seed plot of the Bible" for in it we have, in germ, form, almost all of the great doctrines which are afterwards fully developed in the books of Scripture which follow... Religion/Inspirational Pages 420

The Master Key *by L. W. de Laurence* ISBN: *1-59462-001-6* **$30.95**
In no branch of human knowledge has there been a more lively increase of the spirit of research during the past few years than in the study of Psychology, Concentration and Mental Discipline. The requests for authentic lessons in Thought Control, Mental Discipline and... New Age/Business Pages 422

The Lesser Key Of Solomon Goetia *by L. W. de Laurence* ISBN: *1-59462-092-X* **$9.95**
This translation of the first book of the "Lernegton" which is now for the first time made accessible to students of Talismanic Magic was done, after careful collation and edition, from numerous Ancient Manuscripts in Hebrew, Latin, and French... New Age/Occult Pages 92

Rubaiyat Of Omar Khayyam *by Edward Fitzgerald* ISBN:*1-59462-332-5* **$13.95**
Edward Fitzgerald, whom the world has already learned, in spite of his own efforts to remain within the shadow of anonymity, to look upon as one of the rarest poets of the century, was born at Bredfield, in Suffolk, on the 31st of March, 1809. He was the third son of John Purcell... Music Pages 172

Ancient Law *by Henry Maine* ISBN: *1-59462-128-4* **$29.95**
The chief object of the following pages is to indicate some of the earliest ideas of mankind, as they are reflected in Ancient Law, and to point out the relation of those ideas to modern thought. Religion/History Pages 452

Far-Away Stories *by William J. Locke* ISBN: *1-59462-129-2* **$19.45**
"Good wine needs no bush,' but a collection of mixed vintages does. And this book is just such a collection. Some of the stories I do not want to remain buried for ever in the museum files of dead magazine-numbers an author's not unpardonable vanity..." Fiction Pages 272

Life of David Crockett *by David Crockett* ISBN: *1-59462-250-7* **$27.45**
"Colonel David Crockett was one of the most remarkable men of the times in which he lived. Born in humble life, but gifted with a strong will, an indomitable courage, and unremitting perseverance... Biographies/New Age Pages 424

Lip-Reading *by Edward Nitchie* ISBN: *1-59462-206-X* **$25.95**
Edward B. Nitchie, founder of the New York School for the Hard of Hearing, now the Nitchie School of Lip-Reading, Inc, wrote "LIP-READING Principles and Practice". The development and perfecting of this meritorious work on lip-reading was an undertaking... How-to Pages 400

A Handbook of Suggestive Therapeutics, Applied Hypnotism, Psychic Science ISBN: *1-59462-214-0* **$24.95**
by Henry Munro Health/New Age/Health/Self-help Pages 376

A Doll's House: and Two Other Plays *by Henrik Ibsen* ISBN: *1-59462-112-8* **$19.95**
Henrik Ibsen created this classic when in revolutionary 1848 Rome. Introducing some striking concepts in playwriting for the realist genre, this play has been studied the world over. Fiction/Classics/Plays 308

The Light of Asia *by sir Edwin Arnold* ISBN: *1-59462-204-3* **$13.95**
In this poetic masterpiece, Edwin Arnold describes the life and teachings of Buddha. The man who was to become known as Buddha to the world was born as Prince Gautama of India but he rejected the worldly riches and abandoned the reigns of power when... Religion/History/Biographies Pages 170

The Complete Works of Guy de Maupassant *by Guy de Maupassant* ISBN: *1-59462-157-8* **$16.95**
"For days and days, nights and nights, I had dreamed of that first kiss which was to consecrate our engagement, and I knew not on what spot I should put my lips..." Fiction/Classics Pages 240

The Art of Cross-Examination *by Francis L. Wellman* ISBN: *1-59462-309-0* **$26.95**
Written by a renowned trial lawyer, Wellman imparts his experience and uses case studies to explain how to use psychology to extract desired information through questioning. How-to/Science/Reference Pages 408

Answered or Unanswered? *by Louisa Vaughan* ISBN: *1-59462-248-5* **$10.95**
Miracles of Faith in China Religion Pages 112

The Edinburgh Lectures on Mental Science (1909) *by Thomas* ISBN: *1-59462-008-3* **$11.95**
This book contains the substance of a course of lectures recently given by the writer in the Queen Street Hall, Edinburgh. Its purpose is to indicate the Natural Principles governing the relation between Mental Action and Material Conditions... New Age/Psychology Pages 148

Ayesha *by H. Rider Haggard* ISBN: *1-59462-301-5* **$24.95**
Verily and indeed it is the unexpected that happens! Probably if there was one person upon the earth from whom the Editor of this, and of a certain previous history, did not expect to hear again... Classics Pages 380

Ayala's Angel *by Anthony Trollope* ISBN: *1-59462-352-X* **$29.95**
The two girls were both pretty, but Lucy who was twenty-one who supposed to be simple and comparatively unattractive, whereas Ayala was credited, as her Bombwhat romantic name might show, with poetic charm and a taste for romance. Ayala when her father died was nineteen... Fiction Pages 484

The American Commonwealth *by James Bryce* ISBN: *1-59462-286-8* **$34.45**
An interpretation of American democratic political theory. It examines political mechanics and society from the perspective of Scotsman James Bryce Politics Pages 572

Stories of the Pilgrims *by Margaret P. Pumphrey* ISBN: *1-59462-116-0* **$17.95**
This book explores pilgrims religious oppression in England as well as their escape to Holland and eventual crossing to America on the Mayflower, and their early days in New England... History Pages 268

QTY

The Fasting Cure *by Sinclair Upton*
ISBN: *1-59462-222-1* **$13.95**

In the Cosmopolitan Magazine for May, 1910, and in the Contemporary Review (London) for April, 1910, I published an article dealing with my experiences in fasting. I have written a great many magazine articles, but never one which attracted so much attention... New Age/Self Help/Health Pages 164

Hebrew Astrology *by Sepharial*
ISBN: *1-59462-308-2* **$13.45**

In these days of advanced thinking it is a matter of common observation that we have left many of the old landmarks behind and that we are now pressing forward to greater heights and to a wider horizon than that which represented the mind-content of our progenitors... Astrology Pages 144

Thought Vibration or The Law of Attraction in the Thought World
ISBN: *1-59462-127-6* **$12.95**

by William Walker Atkinson
Psychology/Religion Pages 144

Optimism *by Helen Keller*
ISBN: *1-59462-108-X* **$15.95**

Helen Keller was blind, deaf, and mute since 19 months old, yet famously learned how to overcome these handicaps, communicate with the world, and spread her lectures promoting optimism. An inspiring read for everyone... Biographies/Inspirational Pages 84

Sara Crewe *by Frances Burnett*
ISBN: *1-59462-360-0* **$9.45**

In the first place, Miss Minchin lived in London. Her home was a large, dull, tall one, in a large, dull square, where all the houses were alike, and all the sparrows were alike, and where all the door-knockers made the same heavy sound... Childrens/Classic Pages 88

The Autobiography of Benjamin Franklin *by Benjamin Franklin*
ISBN: *1-59462-135-7* **$24.95**

The Autobiography of Benjamin Franklin has probably been more extensively read than any other American historical work, and no other book of its kind has had such ups and downs of fortune. Franklin lived for many years in England, where he was agent... Biographies/History Pages 332

Name	
Email	
Telephone	
Address	
City, State ZIP	

☐ **Credit Card**   ☐ **Check / Money Order**

Credit Card Number	
Expiration Date	
Signature	

Please Mail to: Book Jungle
PO Box 2226
Champaign, IL 61825
or Fax to: 630-214-0564

ORDERING INFORMATION

web: *www.bookjungle.com*
email: *sales@bookjungle.com*
fax: *630-214-0564*
mail: *Book Jungle PO Box 2226 Champaign, IL 61825*
or PayPal *to sales@bookjungle.com*

Please contact us for bulk discounts

DIRECT-ORDER TERMS

**20% Discount if You Order
Two or More Books**
Free Domestic Shipping!
Accepted: Master Card, Visa,
Discover, American Express